I0710613

The Phoenix Knight

An Epic Fantasy Poem

By Draco Amethystus

Storm Dragon Publishing

The Phoenix Knight: An Epic Fantasy Poem
By Draco Amethystus

Published by Storm Dragon Publishing, LLC.

Copyright © 2024 by Draco Amethystus.

Cover design by Draco Amethystus.

Printed in the United States.

Cataloging-in-Publication Date on file with the Library of Congress.

www.dracoamethystus.com

For all those who were not loved by their loved ones as they should have been.
Remember that love still exists and awaits you.

Introduction

The Phoenix Knight is an epic fantasy poem I wrote in blank verse to honor all those who have not received love where love should have been most freely given. This might have been family, friends, or other loved ones. This might have occurred in childhood or as an adult. Be the circumstances what they may, I have experienced firsthand brave souls who have learned to love well despite never having been taught to do so by someone else in their life. While I hope that this poem will resonate in some manner for all those who read it, this story is first and foremost for them.

Draco Amethystus

Prologue

Books are the realms where human minds may meet

Libraries are book dragons' royal seat

Towers tower over a female shape

Thunderous skies and rain pummel her face

Her cloak, rich with velvet and deep purple

Is no match for the summer storm's deluge

She rushes to the towering towers

Great, oaken doors stand guard…yet inviting

Under the arch, she stops suddenly there

The doors are carved with ancient runes, etched deep

Is it just her or do they glow dimly…

A finger's caress traces the carvings

Magic, perhaps real, travels up her hand

It gently floats on each and every vein

She lets the thought go with a cold shiver

Pulling hard on the door with bated breath

She squeezes past the oaken sentinel

And once more finds her breath taken away

Storm Dragon Library and its treasures

Await impatiently to share their words

Countless books and stories whisper to her

Of adventures hidden in their pages

So much treasure to explore, to dance with

With which to sing a song as one being

Books are worlds within worlds, a multiverse

These are her beliefs and musings of books

And then a rainbow light falls on her face

Her mesmerized state reaches new heights now

She gazes up at the kaleidoscope

Stained glass windows show their love, warm and bright

Depictions of mythical creatures glow

Telling their stories of might, blood, and tears

Flaming colors bask her in their glory

Peace opens her arms wide for an embrace

Stories are havens for the weary mind

Bringing healing to all of humankind

Chapter 1

Books know human hearts better than we do

Few friends or loved ones are ever so true

As she stands still, engulfed in the warm glow

Of so many stories, books, and soft lights

A hooded figure approaches, gentle

Robes of darkest brown rustle and whisper

Whispered words flow from the depths of the hood

She leans in and discerns the inquiry

The question, simple but prevalent still

She replies in the same hushed, quiet tone

The librarian nods without more words

No voice or eloquence necessary

She smiles in return, silence a sweet gift

The monk holds up a hand and beckons on

Enchanted, she follows in his footsteps

Curiosity bubbles in her mind

The scent of parchment calling her to search

But they arrive at their destination

Each tomb encases a life to be shared

No two the same, each unique, none compared

Chapter 2

Dreams arise from stories told and untold

But tales in books are for all to behold

It all feels like a dream, a reverie

Time slows down to a drip, to drops of sand

The beauty before her just overwhelms

No words wish to pass beyond her closed lips

They have arrived at a giant table

It's round and worn, oaken gold in color

Swirling symbols dance across the surface

Each etched in careful perfection and love

Sudden light from above catches her eye

Looking up, a gasp escapes from her lips

She drinks in the rainbow captured in glass

Stories in shades of colors, dark and bright

Encased in that glass are creatures of lore

Vibrant and fiery is the phoenix

Painted in golden orange and fire red

Crowned in the deepest of royal purple

The burning bird of prey cries silently

Locked in combat with a darker figure

One made of mist and murky hues of gray

A stryx, feathered death on wings of midnight

Their talons reach for a deadly embrace

Each is beauty eternalized in glass

One of fire, blood, and lava eruptions

One of the pit's darkness and moon's halo

Time lays forgotten as she watches them

Forever about to shred into flesh

A battle never to be begotten

A coming war always to be promised

Forces battle from within and without

The drums beat threatening faith's doubt and drought

Chapter 3

Stories mirror life's truths, both big and small

But their power may leave you in a sprawl

Her reverie is broken by footsteps

Soft and light but still she hears them approach

The robed librarian smiles so faintly

As he lays a giant tomb down gently

She whispers her thanks as he stands aside

She moves forward to peer at the dark tomb

As she does, the librarian returns

A chair in hand for her to sit and read

A smile of gratitude beams on her face

He returns the smile and a slight nod too

Before leaving her alone to the book

A world soon to be opened up to her

Awe lightens her face along with the smile

As she stares at the cover of the book

The tomb is leather bound, locked with a clip

On a belt wrapping around the cover

The book is filled with an ancient wonder

And yet, gold filigree still shines boldly.

On each page, combating an age's thick dust

An antique treasure sits here before her

She unlocks the clip and opens the book

Illustrious illustrations greet her

And gothic letters invite her to read

The title: Ravçe-el the Phoenix Knight

Like Alice falling down the rabbit hole

All books transport your very heart and soul

Chapter 4

Many stories begin in old castles

But the heroes still endure such hassles

Ravçe-el lives in a cliff-side castle

Overlooking the sea and a river

The only child of the king and the queen

Her life is nothing like a fairy tale

The first king, her true father, had passed on

And her mother, the queen, had remarried

No memories remained of her father

But her mother told her stories at times

The new king is a monster in the dark

Who walks in the daylight and smiles poison

He wears facades of righteous dignity

And quotes scripture for his own vanity

The king locks Ravçe-el in a tower

Left alone with only books for her friends

They teach her about the wide world outside

Providing her wings in her dreams at least

On the rare occasion she is let out

It's to abuse her over and over

Each torture new, creative, and unique

His dark imagination has no bounds

All in the kingdom know of the abuse

But the queen lives in denial of it

And refuses to assist her daughter

Leaving her to hate and an empty cell

Many fairy tales are dark and twisted

The names of the victims left unlisted

Chapter 5

Freedom comes in many shapes and sizes

Even on raven wing as it rises

Years pass in her tower isolation

But then one day a visitor arrives

Not by the door but by the windowsill

A lone raven who can speak her language

The raven and Ravçe-el become friends

Trauma and passion both play a role in

Their building friendship and mutual love

They're able to share and care so much truth

From that day on the raven comes daily

To visit with his friend in the tower

And with time he even builds a nest there

Making himself a new home in the sky

They share so much between their loving souls

Ravçe-el reads books and stories aloud

To the raven who in return tells her

Of the greater and wider world abroad

At night the raven nestles in his nest

While Ravçe-el lays down on her straw bed

Warm thoughts of her friendship providing hope

And beauty where once was only despair

Friends are made between sharing souls, not blood

Family comes from dust, or even mud

<u>Chapter 6</u>

Nothing lasts forever, all has an end

But we still don't know what's around the bend

For the first time in her life, time flies by

Ravçe-el does not take it for granted

But drinks in every moment with her friend

Loving both their talks and their tower home

Yet, all things come to an end, good and ill

One day, unbeknownst to her, the king comes

And listens quietly at the door to

Her conversations with her raven friend

Realizing what's occurring, he storms in

In a fit of rage too swift to be seen

He snatches up the raven in hand and

Breaks his neck, the king's eyes gleaming with glee

Ravçe-el, in shock and grief, lies frozen

Tears flooding her cheeks with all of her pain

As her stepfather flings the dead raven

Landing in her lap, no more sweet stories

The king slithers forward as if a snake

As he spits on her and curses her name

He promises her only living death

Never to see the wider world beyond

Still in a rage, he grabs her books, each one

Piling them in the middle of the room

He builds a blazing bonfire of them all

And in one fell swoop kills all of her joy

The death of imagination is worse

Than many other kinds of cruel curse

Chapter 7

Without another word, the king departs

Having murdered one but killing two hearts

Slamming the door to the tower closed, locked

Ravçe-el, in tears, remains on her knees

Guarding the cold and lifeless body of

Her only and dearest friend, the raven

While the warmth of the fire mocks her with heat

Tis a blaze that can never repeat or

Restore the friendship the king has taken

Torn away like pollen on a fierce wind

Up in smoke goes her imagination

Yet she is flooded with tears of despair

Sobs racking her body, inundated

Rocking askance to a death lullaby

Snuffed out are all the colors of the world

The banner of love ne'er again unfurled

<h1 style="text-align:center"><u>Chapter 8</u></h1>

The flames burn bright in the funeral pyre

Each forked dagger glimmers in that death fire

Finally, the stabbing pain of loss dims

Turning into a throbbing ache, a drum

Beating to the rhythm of her broken heart

As she still holds the body of her friend

She is ready at last to release him

Gently as she can before the great flames

She lays the raven in a burning grave

Where his form is engulfed and devoured

Goodbyes are always painful company

They gobble up loved ones with gluttony

Chapter 9

At the end it feels like the beginning

We're met with Life or Death, but both grinning

Ravçe-el sits and stares into the flames

An obsidian thought occurs to her

Neither life nor death have any meaning

There's no point to any of it at all

Choosing death is the only choice left her

One last freedom, her decision, alone

She stands up with poised resolution, deep

And prepares to walk into her death pyre

In the end there's just one thing left to do

Wait, or make the end happen, swift and true

Chapter 10

Sometimes magic reaches out, just a touch

And fills our lives with more, so very much

A moment before Ravçe-el steps up

And flings herself into the raging fire

She notes a change in the flickering flames

They've begun to shimmer other colors

The normal oranges and reds give way

To brilliant flashes of gold and rich red

A crimson red, fading to light purple

Deepening to a royal violet

Mesmerized by all the changing colors

Her dark thoughts begin to lighten, like dawn

A new hope flares to life in her bosom

Healing light has taken root in her heart

Healing and hope are often together

Flying as one like birds of a feather

Chapter 11

From the ashes, new life is born once more

This new life is one never seen before

Enthralled by the colors, the voice shocks her

It flows out of the fire, a burning bush

A cry follows, a raven's caw and call

And there in the flames, stands her dearest friend

There's a change though in her sweet corvid friend

For he's no longer black, but rather white

Pure, creamy feathers of strong ivory

Mark the power of the reborn raven

Tears fill her eyes once more, but these of joy

The raven speaks to her from the death pyre

"My dear one, there is no more need for tears.

We are reunited, my lovely one."

"And we may remain together longer.

All you must do is join me in the fire."

Fear lurches up in her throat at the thought

Despite her violent plans of before

The kind caress of her friend's calm voice though

Soothes her fear and quiets her rolling mind

Ravçe-el inhales, gathering courage

And walks swiftly into the arms of fire

Actions may be the same on the surface

But beneath skin there's another purpose

Chapter 12

Fire destroys with its burning bright, hot flame

But it also brings new life, all the same

The fire burns brighter as she enters it

The colors shimmer and glimmer faster

She can't see the raven, but she hears him

"You must join with the fire, you must be one."

Ravçe-el doesn't understand at first

But her friend continues to explain it

"Don't resist, but rather let it all in.

It won't destroy, but will give you new life."

Ravçe-el realizes that her teeth are

Clenched and her shoulders tight as she battles

To stop the fire from burning her to ash

But her friend's words seep deep into her soul

Ravçe-el closes her eyes to focus

She imagines all her hate flowing out

Burned to nothing but smoke, soon to disperse

She envisions the fire in her chest

Ravçe-el isn't certain at first but

Soon recognizes there is cooler air

Where the flames of fire once burned so brightly

When her eyes open, it's to snuffed out fire

The white raven flies up to her shoulder

Perching there on her bare but unburned skin

She sees this and looks down at her body

One free of clothing and trauma, reborn

Now is the time to act and change your life

Now is all you have to end pain and strife

Chapter 13

New beginnings will need new locations

From proven abuses and pervasions

The fire is all ash and gone, extinguished

But Ravçe-el can still feel it burning

Inside her chest and through her whole body

Holding her hand up she sees it dancing

Before she can turn to ask her friend though

She hears the pounding steps outside her door

The king heard something and is coming now

Ravçe-el hears the anger in each step

Panic rises in her throat, strangling

The raven calls to her from the window

And realization settles in her mind

She can no longer live her life like this

The king roars as he pounds at the oak door

Ravçe-el hears the chant of keys clinking

She's out of time and forever awaits

Like a key in a lock, an open door

She can almost hear the lock click in place

And the panic simmers, dissipating

A new sensation takes its place inside

The fire has ignited her anger now

That anger turns to will as she desires

And she knows what to do in that moment

Her stepfather's distorted face gnashing

Teeth and spittle through the bars of her door

Ravçe-el walks calmly to the oak door

She raises her hand and flames shoot forward

The fire eats hungerly at the king's beard

His anguished screams are music to her ears

Her friend caws her name, drawing her away

From the door and to the window, freedom

Awaits them there calling both of their names

With the taste of wind and the smell of sun

Ravçe-el is faced once more with doubt though

Looking out over the heights…and the drop

Deadly in its depths, cold in its embrace

Fear rises again in her chest and throat

The raven caws anew to urge courage

And says, "You must welcome in the phoenix

And become one with it, the heat and fire.

Then you will be able to fly like me."

Ravçe-el's ears protest this news at first

But her heart knows the burning truth of it

And just as the oaken door flies open

So too does Ravçe-el fly, far away

An old life ends and a new one begins

A fresh start awaits and gone are the sins

Chapter 14

Beauty is in the eye as we decide

But be open and it can never hide

Glory abounds both in the land and sea

Both in the green forest and the river

Running and glistening in the summer

Sky and sun blending their beauties as one

Even as Ravçe-el looks behind her

On the fiery wings of a phoenix

Hues of purple, gold, sedona, and red

She sees even beauty in the castle

Distance and time will grant a gift, healings

Washed clean is the sharpness of such feelings

Chapter 15

All fires will burn themselves out in their time

Their death is a part of life's rhythm and rhyme

Ravçe-el and the raven fly far fast

But the phoenix tires quickly and fades soon

Her energy and fire burning quite low

As the sun dips below the horizon

The phoenix crash lands near the dark river

Forest surrounds them on every side

The raven calls his friend, but she can't hear

Consciousness has slipped into a darkness

Sleep is where the mind greets every dream

But wakefulness is where they all will teem

Chapter 16

Darkness drapes her in midnight dreamless sleep

She makes not a sound, not one little peep

Ravçe-el wakes up to night's deep darkness

A fire burns and she's draped in a blanket

She's in human form once more, no phoenix

The only flames of the nearby campfire

A tiny figure hops in front of her

Her friend, the raven, a feather's light touch

Against her cool cheek, a lovely comfort

She smiles sleepily and sits up slowly

That's when the fear returns full and plenty

A large outline glowing gold sits nearby

The fire making the gleam of the armor

Shine like a fallen star in her campsite

Before she stands to fight, the raven speaks

"You were cold and without flame. I found help."

The man, for tis a man, whispers a word

And more dreamless sleep falls deep upon her

Despite one's strength, we all have some weakness

We're special but that's not a uniqueness

Chapter 17

Morning dawns with bright, shining, golden rays

A true knight waits to show her other ways

She wakes this time to golden sun and knight

He speaks not but only nods his greeting

And she's grateful for his quiet kindness

Ravçe-el needs a moment of silence

The knight seems to understand and allows

Her as much time as she needs, not speaking

Only working on the dying embers

Making a breakfast of bacon and eggs

Silently, he hands her a plate gently

She mumbles a thank you and shares her food

With the raven, her friend, who nibbles it

And they both watch the knight who eats as well

When their bellies are full, she goes to speak

But the knight takes her plate and hands her clothes

They're in a bundle and she almost cries

At the kindness of this stranger, her first

Ravçe-el walks with her friend to the woods

And changes into the knight's gift, the clothes

Clearly, they are his, much too large for her

But she rolls up the pants and the shirt sleeves

When she returns to the campfire, there's more

A package of food is waiting for her

Placed in her seat by the great golden knight

Tears of gratitude fall from her eyes now

Ravçe-el clears her throat to give her thanks

"Thank you so much for all of your kindness.

How can I ever repay you for this?"

The golden knight smiles a beautiful smile

"You need pay me nothing. You were in want.

This is what knights do, they help those in need."

Ravçe-el has never known such kindness

Her heart and her mind don't know what to do

The knight seems to know her thoughts as if words

"You have not had much kindness in your life.

But I can promise if you provide it

For others, the world will be much better."

"And if you should ever wish to know more

About being a knight, just ask for me.

All know where I reside, the golden knight."

With these words he mounts his horse and rides off

Ravçe-el and the raven remain there

Enjoying the dying embers of fire

Percolating on the words of the knight

Wondering what their next steps shall be now

After some quiet discussion, they choose

To walk to the city nearby and see

What a new life there might offer them both

And so they set out on the road, hopeful

New horizons are never really new

Yet each has its color, a unique hue

Chapter 18

Time flows by like meandering rivers

Time, the god of both takers and givers

Years pass by in that blinding way of time

Sneaking up on you without you knowing

But these years are saturated with joy

Brimming full till they sweetly overflow

Ravçe-el found so much in that city

Assistance, kindness, friendship, and much love

She was given a job in a small store

Filled with books, stories, music, and much more

There she met a handsome man, a hunter

Who loved to read books during those hours

Spent hunting and wandering the forests

Drenching his life in beauty, in and out

It was not long and he knelt before her

Offering her a ring and a shared life

Ravçe-el cried and said yes with more tears

They kissed and were married in that same store

They moved to a forest cottage nearby

And a little girl was born to them there

Growing with sweet golden curls and long locks

Running about with leaves and animals

She builds a shop, an apothecary

Her friend, the white raven, teaches the art

Of healing and herbs little by little

A contentment is draped over their home

Peace is but an interlude between wars

Hiding won't work, there are too many doors

Chapter 19

As day will sing again time after time

So too will night's bells ring their darkly chime

One day Ravçe-el is flying about

Above the world wing in wing with her friend

The white raven bathed in the warming flames

Of phoenix fire flowing from her feathers

A dark arrow bathes the sun in darkness

Ravçe-el looks up and she is blinded

By the rays of the sun and something more

Something devoid of light which slams her hard

She senses feathers, feels the claws, her blood

Pours from the strikes of a wicked sharp beak

Her eyes adjust through the pain and behold

A phoenix opposite, a blackest stryx

Ravçe-el feels the black hole pull of death

The power of a stryx, the lack of light

Eyes of onyx and malice stare her down

As they plummet to the earth, to their deaths

Phoenix and stryx crash into forest trees

Branches bruise and bark scratches as they fall

Finally landing in beds of deep leaves

Returning to human forms in their sleep

As Ravçe-el regains her consciousness

She stands up to face a fierce unknown foe

Only to be rocked once more by old wounds

Before her stands her stepfather, the king

Even old scars and wounds open anew

When past's darkness hunts and haunts us so true

Chapter 20

A dark star has fallen from the night sky

Seeking always to rise again so high

"Hello, my little lost princess," he purrs

And yet, his words slither like a serpent

Across her skin and clouding her judgment

The world is less clear and the sun less bright

"It's been such a long time, my dear princess.

Your mother and I have missed you so much.

She mourned you for dead, but I knew you lived.

Do you wish to know how I knew all this?"

No words will rise up in the ashes of

Her mouth, now only a funeral pyre

Ignited and burned the moment she saw

That her stepfather had found her once more

"Aren't you even a little curious?"

His voice still maintains all that old venom

Mocking her with his false kindness and smile

A thing fit only for thieves and monsters

Ravçe-el knows her stepfather as both

A thief of joy and a killer of dreams

A monster, thirsty to drink up her pain

And to eat up all her self-doubt and fear

That mocking smile widens, showing he knows

Those dark thoughts she has, once her loyal friends

Long gone these many years and reappeared

As if they'd never gone in the first place

"Come now, my little fire bird, my precious."

She can almost see the venom dripping

From his lips and foaming up in his beard

An image of all she hates about him

"Very well. I will explain it to you.

After you so rudely abandoned me…

Not to mention, your poor distraught mother,

I took a much closer look at that fire."

"It seemed to me to be the only way

You could have transformed into a phoenix.

We both know that you possess no magic,

That there is nothing special about you."

"When I realized that the fire had changed you,

I was certain that I could do the same…

I ate the ashes, as much as I could

And now you will see all of my power."

Ravçe-el finds no words before the rant

Of the tyrant who has terrorized her

Most of her life, the monster in her bed

And he grins wickedly at her silence

Ravçe-el has no need for words now though

She will let fire and talons speak for her

And in bursts of flames a phoenix is born

Raging in glowing hues of red and gold

The monstrous smile never leaves the king's face

As he's wrapped in shadows and grayest mists

The stryx, born of darkness, cries for battle

And thus begins their legendary war

The maneuvers made and blood shed that day

Can never be truly captured in words

Nor shared fully within a book's covers

But know this, their fight was long and bloody

Ravçe-el and the king both had great wounds

Finally, she was able to trap him

Between large branches of a giant oak

And he lay there, unmoving and near death

As Ravçe-el moves forward to kill him

Her friend, the white raven, cautions mercy

Concerned for her soul more than for the king's

Something already rotten and decayed

Through bloody lips and a dark smile, he speaks

His final words on that grim battlefield

"I promise, I will never stop my search

To find you and kill you, my dear daughter."

With a sinister smile of her own make

Ravçe-el responds in kind to the king

"I will always be ready to fight you,

But know this, I was never your daughter."

Even the fiercest fights do not end war

When one combatant must finish the score

Chapter 21

One final piece to share in our story

Of futures unknown, not of great glory

I wish I could share a happy ending

But I don't want to ever lie to you

Ravçe-el and her stepfather the king

Continued their battles for many years

They passed into legend with fading time

The king raised an army of dark shadows

And Ravçe-el joined the golden knight's court

Fighting by him and all his greatest knights

But these stories are only that, stories

They're legends, myths, tales of forgotten times

There's no truth to them as scholars tell us

So, just enjoy them as they are, stories

Stories never really have any ends

They only have sharp curves and endless bends

<u>Epilogue</u>

Stories hold more truths than most ever know

Here's a hint though, truths will set you aglow

Tears roll down her cheeks as she finishes

The story of the Phoenix Knight, so brave

So true, so bright, always ready to fight

For those who had no voice, stripped by others

She closes the book tenderly, gentle

Caressing the care worn leather cover

With her fingers light and soft, whispering

Gratitude and love for this precious book

A hand at her side offers a kerchief

She smiles sweetly at the librarian

Taking the tissue with trembling hands

She nods her thanks and wipes away her tears

The librarian smiles in return and

Retrieves the tomb of ancient lore from her

Clutching her shoulder on last time before

Walking away into shadows of stacks

The woman stands and prepares herself for

The storm outside and all its thundering

And the lightning dancing to its own tune

That she may hold it as never before

While stories may never come to an end

Our time together is complete, my friend